Boonedoggie

By

Arvil Wiley

Illustrated by

Heather Huffman

One day, a boy named Logan was given a new puppy to take care of and train. Logan's mama asked him if he had a name for the puppy.

Logan thought for a moment and then said, "I think I'll name him Boonedoggie!"

Boonedoggie was very excited to be in his new home. He was so excited in fact that the first thing he did was squat down and tinkle on the living room floor.

"Uh-oh!" Logan shouted. "Look what Boonedoggie just did! He's a bad dog!"

"It's okay Logan," his mama said with a smile. "Boonedoggie is just a puppy and will have to learn not to go in the house. It's your job now to teach him. Make sure you take him out often so he will learn."

"I know. It won't happen again," Logan answered as he carried a squirming Boonedoggie outside.

The next day Logan awoke to find that Boonedoggie had put one of his favorite shoes in his mouth and gnawed on it all night because he thought it was a chew toy.

"No!" shouted Logan. "Bad dog!"

Logan told his mama that Boonedoggie ruined his shoe but she just smiled, asked Logan why he didn't put his shoes away, and reminded him that Boonedoggie was just a puppy that needed lots of attention.

That same afternoon, Logan was sitting on the porch eating a hot dog for lunch. He took one bite and then set it aside to get a drink of soda. When he reached for the hot dog to get another bite, he found that Boonedoggie had snatched it from his plate and quickly ran behind a bush to hide.

Logan yelled for his mama, but she just smiled, asked him if he had fed Boonedoggie, and reminded him once again that Boonedoggie was just a puppy and didn't know any better.

Later that evening, Logan took Boonedoggie outside
to play in the back yard. The first thing Boonedoggie
did was run over to a mud hole to take a long drink, and
then he decided he wanted to start rolling around in
the mud.

"No Boonedoggie! Not again!" Logan squawked.

When Logan told his mama what happened she just smiled and asked him if he had given Boonedoggie some fresh water to drink.

"No, I guess I forgot!" Logan shrieked as Boonedoggie hastily shook mud all over him.

"You better give that dog a bath Logan, and you need one too! Be patient with Boonedoggie and remember that he's just a puppy!" Logan's mama said.

After Logan gave Boonedoggie a bath, the two of them got ready for bed. Logan made sure that all of his shoes were off the floor and in the closet. He also made sure that Boonedoggie had gone outside to potty.

The next morning, Logan was awakened by Boonedoggie licking his face. He told his mama that Boonedoggie slobbered all over him, but she just laughed, told Logan to wash his face, and said that's how puppies show affection.

Later that morning, Logan let Boonedoggie outside to run around and play while he stayed inside to put food and fresh water in his doggie bowls. A little while later, Logan heard his mama screaming. It seems that she had just caught Boonedoggie as he finished digging up some of her favorite flowers.

"No Boonedoggie!" she yelled. "Bad dog!"

Logan ran outside to see what happened. He looked over at his mama with a big smile then ran back into the house to find an empty vase.

Logan returned with the vase and asked his mama not to be angry at Boonedoggie because, after all, he was just a puppy. Her scowl quickly turned into a smile as she and Logan began to laugh. She told Logan that it's good to forgive and that forgiving others is pleasing to God.

"Really?" Logan asked, "How many more times should we keep forgiving Boonedoggie? Seven times?"

"More like seven times seventy," his mama said as she began arranging the uprooted flowers in the vase.

"Whoa! That's a lot of times!" replied Logan.

Logan's mama looked at him and explained, "Seven times seventy is just a big number, and all it really means is that we ought to be kindhearted and always willing to forgive others even when we don't feel like it. We should also forgive those rascals like Boonedoggie even if we think he doesn't deserve it."

"That sounds pretty hard. I don't know if he deserves it with the way he's been behaving, and I don't know if I have that much patience," a puzzled Logan said.

"Sure you can Logan!" his mama declared. "You know what? We don't deserve God's love, favor, and forgiveness either, and we can never earn it. He gives it to us freely because He always loves us no matter what. Even when we fall short, He never stops loving us and never gives up on us."

"Wow! That makes me feel pretty special!" Logan exclaimed as he cuddled with his playful puppy.

"Do you know who else loves us no matter what?"
Logan asked.

"Who's that?" his mama answered with a grin.

"BOONEDOGGIE!!!" Logan shouted as the two of them raced across the yard.

The End

Made in the USA
Columbia, SC
08 December 2021

50734855R00015